Lizzie
the Sweet Treats
Fairy

Special thanks to
Narinder Dhami

ISBN 978-0-545-43394-5

12 11 10 9 8 7 6 5 4 3 2 1   12 13 14 15 16 17/0

Printed in the U.S.A.   40

First Scholastic printing, August 2012

Lizzie

the Sweet Treats Fairy

by Daisy Meadows

SCHOLASTIC INC.

New York   Toronto   London   Auckland
Sydney   Mexico City   New Delhi   Hong Kong

The Fairyland Palace

The Orangery

The Lake

Maze

Petting Zoo

PETTING ZOO

Garden

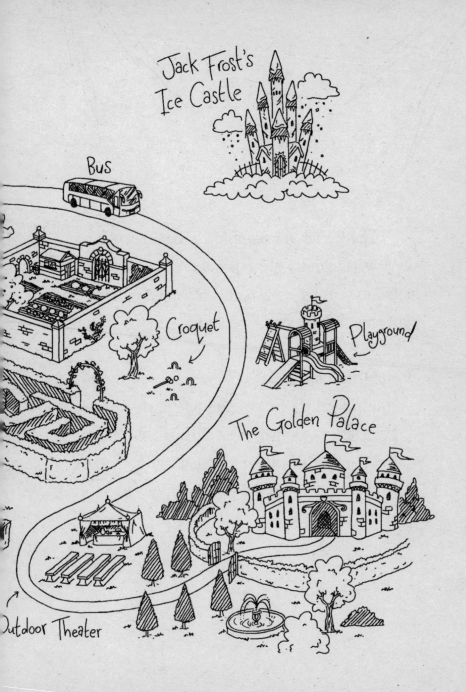

The fairies are planning a magical ball,
With guests of honor and fun for all.
They're expecting a night full of laughter and cheer,
But they'll get a shock when my goblins appear!

Adventures and treats will be things of the past,
And I'll beat those troublesome fairies at last.
My iciest magic will blast through the room
And the world will be plunged into grimness
and gloom!

Contents

Royal Tea Party

"Having a tea party in the Orangery is going to be really fun!" Rachel exclaimed to her best friend, Kirsty. "I bet that's just what the *real* princes and princesses who once lived in the Golden Palace used to do."

"I wonder if we're going to have a royal tea with cucumber sandwiches and cupcakes," Kirsty said with a smile. "The Orangery is the perfect place for a special party!"

The Orangery was a pretty white greenhouse with huge arched windows. It stood on the grounds of the Golden Palace. Terra-cotta pots of orange, lemon, and lime trees lined the walls of the Orangery, and the air was warm

and smelled like citrus. A spiral staircase in the middle of the building swept up to a wrought-iron balcony that had spectacular views of the Golden Palace and its enormous grounds. From the balcony, Rachel and Kirsty could see the drawbridge and moat, the lake and gardens, the maze, the petting zoo, and the croquet field.

"The Golden Palace looks beautiful in the sunshine," Kirsty remarked. The palace had four high towers, one at each corner of the building, and a fifth tower, the highest one, right in the center. Flags flew on top of all five towers and their golden turrets glittered in the glowing spring sun.

"Aren't we lucky to be here for the Royal Sleepover Camp?" Rachel smiled at Kirsty as they made their way back down the spiral staircase. "Thank you *so* much for inviting me to come."

The Golden Palace was located in the countryside near Kirsty's hometown of Wetherbury, and the girls were spending spring vacation there with a group of other kids, doing all kinds of fun and interesting activities.

"Gather around, kids," called Louis, one of the camp directors. "Caroline and I are going to show you how to set the table for a tea party fit for a prince or a princess!"

Rachel and Kirsty hurried over to join the others. The ground floor of the Orangery was set up with tables and chairs, ready for the tea party.

"OK, the first things we need are

snow-white tablecloths," Louis announced. Rachel, Kirsty, and the other kids watched as he and Caroline shook out a heavy linen tablecloth and placed it on one of the tables, smoothing out the creases.

"And now for matching napkins,"
Caroline said with a smile. She took
one of the napkins and, with several
swift folds, turned it into a fan. She
folded the second napkin into a pretty

flower shape, and
the kids laughed
and applauded.
"That looks
complicated!"
Rachel whispered to
Kirsty with a grin.

Louis and Caroline added shiny
silverware, plates with a flower pattern,
dishes, teacups, and saucers to the table,
as well as a tiered cake stand. The
finishing touch was a little glass vase
containing a single pink rose.

"Oh, this all looks beautiful!" Rachel

sighed. "I can just imagine a princess holding a tea party here, wearing her dressiest gown."

"Don't forget we might meet a *fairy* princess today, Rachel!" Kirsty whispered in her ear.

All week long, the girls had been helping their new friends, the Princess Fairies, search for their magical tiaras. On the day they arrived at the Golden Palace, Rachel and Kirsty had been thrilled to receive an invitation to attend a Fairyland ball. But Jack Frost and his goblins had crashed the party and had stolen the Princess Fairies' tiaras, taking them to the human world. In the nick of time, Queen Titania's magic spell had made sure that the tiaras would end up somewhere in the Golden Palace. This

way, the girls could help their fairy
friends find them and take them back to
Fairyland.

"OK, now it's your turn, guys," Louis
called. "Everything you need is on those
tables by the windows."

Rachel and Kirsty
went to collect a
tablecloth and
some napkins.
Then they began
to set their table,
along with everyone else.

"I know we've found four of the magic
tiaras so far," Rachel said in a low
voice as she and Kirsty spread out the
tablecloth. "But it's so important that we
find them all!"

Kirsty nodded seriously. Both girls

knew that the Princess Fairies didn't just need their tiaras to look after their own special kind of magic—the tiaras affected *all* fairy magic. Without them, no one in either the fairy or the human world would have a happy or magical time ever again.

Caroline came over and showed Rachel and Kirsty how to make flower and fan shapes with their napkins. Then the girls carefully laid out their plates and silverware.

"There!" Kirsty placed a little vase containing a white rose on the table and stood back to admire it. "What do you think, Rachel?"

"It looks great," Rachel said, "but let's polish the silverware to make sure it really shines."

She glanced around and spotted some cloths on one of the side tables next to a display of silver serving dishes. Then, to Rachel's surprise, she noticed that one of the serving dishes was sparkling especially brightly.

"Kirsty!" Rachel tugged gently at her friend's arm. "Look over there. See that serving dish?"

"I see it!" Kirsty whispered with excitement. "Could that be fairy magic?"

"Let's find out!" Rachel replied.

The girls hurried over to the serving dish and stood in front of it so that no one else could see. Then Rachel lifted the domed lid. There, on the silver tray, sat a tiny fairy.

Kirsty gasped. "It's Princess Lizzie the Sweet Treats Fairy!"

Roses and Cupcakes

Lizzie jumped to her feet and waved up at the girls. She wore a bright yellow dress and strappy pink sandals. But she was dusted from head to toe with what looked like powdered sugar and flour.

"Hello, girls," Lizzie whispered, a big smile on her face. "I was hoping you'd find me!"

"Why are you so dusty, Lizzie?" asked Rachel as the little fairy brushed off her clothes.

"I've been in the palace kitchen searching for my tiara," Lizzie explained. "I'm sure it's there *somewhere*! Will you help me look? Otherwise, you won't have any wonderful treats for your tea party."

"Of course we'll help," Kirsty told her.

At that moment, Caroline clapped her hands to get everyone's attention. Rachel and Kirsty turned to look, shielding Lizzie from sight.

"Louis and I think all of your tables

are great," Caroline announced. "The Orangery looks beautiful. Now it's time to prepare the food for the tea party, so we're going over to the palace kitchen."

"But first you need these," Louis added. He and Caroline began handing out white chef's hats and aprons.

"Good, we're going to the kitchen!" Kirsty murmured to Rachel as they put on their hats and aprons. "That means we'll be able to look for Lizzie's tiara."

"Hooray!" Lizzie exclaimed, looking

excited. She dove
into the pocket
of Rachel's
apron and
ducked down
out of sight.
Then Louis and
Caroline led the way
out of the Orangery toward the kitchen
door at the back of the Golden Palace.
Rachel and Kirsty followed along with
everyone else. But just as Caroline was
about to pull the back door open, they
all heard a loud wail of disappointment
from inside.

"Oh, no! That wasn't supposed to
happen!"

Wondering what was going on,
everyone, including the girls, rushed

into the kitchen. There they found Mrs. King, the kind palace cook, staring down at the cake pan she was holding. Inside was what looked like a pancake.

"Are you all right, Mrs. King?" asked Louis.

Mrs. King shook her head. She looked close to tears. "This is supposed to be a chocolate soufflé," she explained, "But  look!" She held out the cake pan. "It should have risen in the oven so it would look light and fluffy—but it's as flat as when I put it in. And the Jell-O didn't set right in the refrigerator, either." Mrs.

King pointed to a bowl of watery red goo on the counter. "Nothing's going right today."

Kirsty and Rachel exchanged a glance. This was all because Lizzie's tiara was missing!

"Oh, poor Mrs. King," said Caroline, patting the flustered cook on the arm. "But *something* smells delicious. What is it?"

Mrs. King brightened a little as she pointed to rows of cupcakes sitting on cooling racks  on the big pine table.

"The cupcakes came out well, at least," she replied. "We'll be able to decorate them for the tea party."

"Lizzie's tiara couldn't have been far away when the cupcakes were baked if they turned out OK!" Kirsty whispered to Rachel, who nodded.

Everyone sat down at the table while Mrs. King gave each pair of kids a job to do. Some of them would be mixing different colors of icing, and some would be making sugar flowers.

As they waited their turn, Rachel and Kirsty gazed around the kitchen, hoping to spot the telltale sparkle of Lizzie's magic tiara. There were mixing bowls, wooden spoons, and baking pans on the countertops, and tea carts were lined up against one of the walls, ready for the party. The door to the pantry stood open. Inside were lots of jars and tins on shelves, and big sacks of sugar and flour on the floor. But they couldn't see the missing tiara anywhere!

"Kirsty and Rachel, you'll be making crystallized rose petals," Mrs. King announced with a smile. "We'll put them on the cakes and scatter them on the cake stands, too."

"Oh, that sounds wonderful!" said Kirsty.

Mrs. King handed Rachel a little basket. "That's the way to the kitchen garden," the cook told the girls, pointing to a door on the other side of the room. "You'll find the rose bushes at the far end of the garden, past the vegetables. Collect as many different-colored petals as you can. Then we'll paint them with egg whites and dust them with sugar."

"They're going to look so pretty!" Rachel remarked as she and Kirsty stepped out the door.

The kitchen garden was neatly planted with several rows of vegetables, herbs, and sweet-scented lavender shrubs. In one corner was a shed with the door open, revealing a collection of gardening tools.

"It smells amazing out here," said Kirsty, sniffing the air.

"Look, there are the roses," Rachel pointed out.

The roses were growing up the tall

trellises at the far end of the kitchen garden. They were covered with fragrant white, pink, and pale yellow blooms, and the girls stopped to admire them for a minute.

"Let's just take one or two petals from some of the flowers," Kirsty suggested. "It seems wrong to pick a whole blossom when they look so pretty growing here."

Rachel nodded as Lizzie fluttered out of her apron pocket and hovered over the roses.

"I'll help, girls!" Lizzie cried.

Rachel and Kirsty got to work,

carefully plucking a petal here and a petal there. Meanwhile, Lizzie sat in the basket and sorted them by their different colors, stacking the petals neatly.

As the girls were working, Kirsty suddenly became aware of gruff voices on the other side of the trellis. She nudged Rachel.

"Who's that?" she asked.

"It might be the gardeners," Rachel replied.

Kirsty stepped up to the trellis, parted the prickly branches of the roses, and peeked through the wooden slats. Her eyes widened when she saw three goblins! They were also dressed in chef's hats and aprons, and they were digging a large and very messy hole.

Beside the goblins was a wheelbarrow full of grass clippings and leaves. Kirsty guessed that the gardeners must have left it behind.

Then Kirsty clapped her hand to her mouth in excitement. She'd spotted Lizzie's missing golden tiara underneath the wheelbarrow! It was leaning against one of the wheels and twinkling brightly in the spring sunshine.

"What is it, Kirsty?" asked Rachel.

"There are three goblins behind the trellis, and they have Lizzie's tiara!" Kirsty whispered.

Lizzie in a Tizzy!

Rachel and Lizzie rushed to look. They could see the tiara glittering in the sunshine.

"This is a perfect hiding place," the biggest goblin bragged as he tossed another shovelful of dirt aside. "No one will ever guess that the tiara's buried in the ground."

"It was *my* idea to bury the tiara," one of the other goblins boasted. "No, it wasn't," the third argued. "It was *my* idea!"

"We have to get the tiara back," Rachel whispered to Lizzie and Kirsty while the goblins were busy arguing. "But we can't reach it from here."

Suddenly Kirsty remembered the garden shed they'd seen earlier. "I have an idea," she whispered to Rachel and Lizzie. "Wait here!"

Kirsty hurried over to the shed, went inside, and saw exactly what she was looking for—a rake. Quickly she grabbed it and then hurried back to Rachel and Lizzie. Kneeling down on their side of the trellis, Kirsty poked the head of the rake through the slats and out the other side.

"Good thinking, Kirsty!" Rachel murmured.

Kirsty carefully moved the rake backward and forward, trying to hook the tiara onto its teeth. But as she was doing so, the rake nudged the wheelbarrow wheel, and it rolled forward slightly. Uh-oh! Kirsty froze as the goblins stopped digging and turned around.

"That's strange," the biggest goblin remarked.

"The wind must have moved it," said one of the others. Then they all started shoveling again. Kirsty breathed a sigh of relief. She tried once more, and this time she managed to snare the tiara with the rake. She began to drag it toward the trellis as quietly as she could.

Suddenly, though, the tiara got stuck on a rose root. Kirsty grumbled in dismay and tugged at the rake, trying

to free the tiara, but it wouldn't budge.
Rachel slid her arm between the slats
and tried to reach out and grab it, but it
wasn't close enough.

"I'll get it, girls," Lizzie whispered.

Rachel and Kirsty
watched as
Lizzie fluttered
through the
slats of the
trellis.

"The hole
should be big
enough now,"
one of the goblins declared, throwing
aside his shovel. "Let's get the tiara."

The girls glanced at each other
anxiously as the goblins walked over to
the wheelbarrow.

"It's gone!" the biggest goblin yelled.
"No, there it is!"
the third goblin
shouted,
pointing at
the tiara stuck
on the rose
root. "And
there's a pesky
fairy after it, too!"

"Quick, we have to help Lizzie now!"
Rachel said urgently to Kirsty. The girls
dashed around the trellis and were just
in time to see the goblins turning over
the wheelbarrow as Lizzie hovered over
the tiara. The leaves and grass clippings
tumbled out of the wheelbarrow and
fell on top of the little fairy, completely
covering her.

"We need to find another hiding place," the big goblin yelled, grabbing the tiara. "And fast!"

As the goblins ran off, Kirsty and Rachel quickly pulled Lizzie out of the pile of leaves and grass.

"Oh, thank you, girls!" Lizzie gasped, shaking a leaf from her hair. "What should we do now? I'm so worried I may never get my beautiful tiara back."

"We won't give up, Lizzie," Rachel replied in a determined voice. "The goblins couldn't have gone very far."

"Maybe we'd better take these rose petals back to Mrs. King," Kirsty suggested. "Then we can think about where we're going to look next."

Lizzie flew to hide in Rachel's apron pocket, and Kirsty picked up the basket

of rose petals. Then they headed back
to the kitchen. But when they arrived,
the girls couldn't believe their eyes. The
three goblins were sitting at the table
along with everyone else, and they
were mixing up an enormous bowl of
green icing!

What a Mess!

"Ah, there you are, girls," said Mrs. King. "Come and sit down. Wash the rose petals carefully, please, and then you can crystallize them."

Rachel and Kirsty hurried to sit down next to the goblins, hoping to find out where they'd hidden Lizzie's tiara this time. The goblins were giggling and enjoying themselves. Their faces were smeared with crumbs. Whenever they thought no one was looking, they would sneak a bite out of one of the delicious cupcakes in front of them. Then they rearranged the cupcakes on the cooling racks so that Mrs. King wouldn't notice.

"Look at me!" said the biggest goblin. He stuck his hand into the bowl and drew a green icing mustache on his face. The other two goblins roared with laughter. Then one of the others scooped out a lump of icing and made himself two long green earrings, which he hung from his big ears. They all laughed even harder.

"I wish we knew what they did with Lizzie's tiara," Rachel whispered to Kirsty. The girls had finished washing the rose petals and were now coating them with egg whites. They were trying to keep a sharp eye on the goblins, but it was hard when they had their own job to do!

Kirsty took a quick glance at the goblins and couldn't help but grin. "Look what they're doing with their cupcakes, Rachel!" she whispered.

Instead of icing their cupcakes separately, the goblins had stuck all the little cakes together in a giant pile and were covering them with thick green icing to make one enormous lopsided cake blob. "What a mess!" Rachel said, frowning as one of the goblins ran his finger around the mixing bowl and licked off the icing.

Kirsty saw Lizzie peeking out of Rachel's pocket and looking worried. "No sign of your tiara yet, Lizzie," Kirsty whispered as she and Rachel dipped their rose petals into a bowl of sugar. "But we'll keep looking."

Soon everyone had finished their preparations. Then Mrs. King, Louis, and Caroline helped everyone decorate the cupcakes with icing, silver balls, sugar flowers, and Rachel and Kirsty's crystallized rose petals. The little cakes looked beautiful when everyone had finished.

"It's time to take the cakes over to the Orangery now," said Mrs. King, glancing at the clock. "The tea party is going to start soon, so we should load everything onto the cart. You've all worked very hard, and the cakes look wonderful!"

Rachel and Kirsty carried their cupcakes over to the cart, as did everyone else—except the goblins. They were fighting over the mixing bowl because they all wanted the leftover icing.

"Well, this is an, um, unusual cake," Mrs. King said, staring at the big messy green blob in front of the goblins. She picked up the cake and placed it on an empty cart.

"No!" the biggest goblin yelled. He jumped up and furiously stomped his foot, grabbing the cart handle. "You can't take our cake—it's a special cake with a special surprise in it!"

Rachel's eyes widened as she realized what the goblin meant. "I can guess *exactly* what the special surprise is," Rachel whispered to Kirsty. "The goblins hid Lizzie's tiara in their cake!"

Cart Dash!

Kirsty nodded. "They must have put the tiara in the middle of the cupcakes and then quickly covered it with icing when we weren't looking!" she whispered. "We can't let Mrs. King take it to the Orangery."

Rachel hurried over to the cook. "Maybe the boys think their cake needs a little more work," she suggested.

"Kirsty and I could help them finish it up, and then we can bring it over to the Orangery in a little while."

"That's a good idea," Mrs. King agreed. "Come along then, the rest of you. Let's wheel these carts over to the Orangery."

Rachel and Kirsty waited as Louis and Caroline held the kitchen doors open. Everyone followed Mrs. King out, wheeling their carts with them. Now the only cart left in the kitchen was the one with the goblins' green cake on it.

The goblins were still grabbing the

mixing bowl from
one another and
trying to scrape
out the last bits
of icing for
themselves.
They didn't even

notice that everyone except Rachel and
Kirsty had left the kitchen.

"Good work, girls," Lizzie called,
flying out of the pocket of Rachel's
apron. "Now let's get my tiara back!"
She zoomed over to the goblins, who
shrieked with rage as soon as they
spotted her.

"We know where you hid my tiara,"
Lizzie said. "And we'd like it back!"

"No way!" yelled the biggest goblin.
The three of them jumped up from their

chairs and ran across the kitchen, taking the cart and the cake with them.

"Help me catch them, girls!" Lizzie yelled. She zoomed around Rachel and Kirsty and showered them with fairy dust from her wand. Instantly, the girls shrank down to fairy-size. Fluttering their glittery wings, the friends started to chase the goblins.

The three goblins were swerving around the enormous kitchen with the cart. They were bumping into everything as they raced around, knocking into all the hanging copper pots and pans so they clanged loudly. Then they banged into the table, tipping over two chairs and a bowl of pink icing. The bowl crashed to the floor, spilling icing everywhere. Even though

Lizzie and the girls did their best to
catch up with the goblins by darting
back and forth, they didn't have a
chance of getting the tiara.

"Keep moving!" the biggest goblin
shouted to the other two. "Those pesky
fairies can't do a thing if we keep on
running!"

"He's right," Kirsty panted. "We're just flying around in circles! How are we going to stop them?"

Lizzie was hovering over a puddle of pink icing on the kitchen floor. She stared down at it thoughtfully.

"We know how greedy the goblins are," Lizzie said. "They love the icing and the cakes. Maybe we can use that to stop them and get my tiara back." She flew down to the table and pointed at one of the piping bags that was filled with icing. "Give me a hand, please, Rachel!"

Rachel and Lizzie lifted up the bag

between them and waited for the goblins
to pass by with the cart. Then they
aimed the bag at the biggest goblin and
pressed down hard. Dark blue icing
squirted out of the bag and hit the
goblin right in the face!

"Stop that!" the goblin roared. But
then he licked a little bit of the icing off

with his tongue. "Scrumptious," he said, stopping to lick *all* the icing off his face. Meanwhile, Kirsty had spotted a jar of silver balls open on the table. She waited until the other two goblins ran past with the cart, then she dumped the jar out. The balls spilled all over the floor.

"What's happening?" the second goblin squealed as he slid on the silver balls. "The floor's all slippery!" He tried to regain his balance but ended up on his bottom.

Now there was only one goblin left pushing the cart around the kitchen.

Rachel wondered how to stop him, but then she remembered how the goblins had covered Lizzie with the leaves and grass from the wheelbarrow. That gave her an idea. She swooped down toward the trolley and grabbed a chunk of cake from the goblins' green creation as the cart sped toward her.

"Look, I have yummy cake!" Rachel called, waving it in front of the goblin's nose. "Would you like some? Or should I eat it all myself?"

"Give it to me!" the goblin demanded, licking his lips.

"Then come and get it," Rachel replied. She flew over to the pantry and through the open door, where she hovered above the sacks of flour and sugar that lay on the floor. The goblin raced into the pantry after her, his eyes fixed greedily on the chunk of cake Rachel was holding. At the last possible moment, Rachel zoomed up into the air out of reach and the goblin crashed the cart into the sacks, splitting them open. A large white cloud

of flour dust burst into the air.

"I can't see a thing!" the goblin complained, coughing and spluttering. "Where did that fairy go with my cake?"

"Nice work, girls!" Lizzie cried. "Now we just have to find my tiara!"

A Magical Cake

Lizzie swooped down and picked up a spoon from the table. Rachel and Kirsty did the same. Then the three of them fluttered over to the cake on the cart. Using the spoons like shovels, they began to dig through the gloopy green icing and lumps of spongy cake.

Suddenly Kirsty spotted something

glittering in the middle of the cupcake mess.

"I can see the tiara!" she exclaimed, digging away with her spoon.

A few moments later, all the cake and icing had been scraped away to reveal Lizzie's golden tiara. Although it had lots of sweet stickiness on it, the tiara still had a magical shimmer. Rachel and Kirsty smiled at each other in delight.

"I'm so happy to have my tiara back!" Lizzie said with a sigh. With one twirl of her wand, she quickly cleaned the tiara and it shrank down to fairy-size.

Lizzie picked it up carefully and placed it on her head while Rachel and Kirsty clapped and cheered.

"We lost the tiara!" grumbled the biggest goblin, "and now I feel sick, too!"

"Me, too," the second goblin agreed. "My tummy hurts!"

"We ate too many sweet treats," the third goblin groaned, holding his stomach. Complaining loudly, all three goblins stomped outside.

Lizzie, Rachel, and Kirsty couldn't help laughing.

"Maybe they won't be so greedy next time!" Rachel remarked.

"Girls, I can't thank you enough," Lizzie cried. "I can't wait to get back to Fairyland and tell everyone how wonderful you were. But first" — 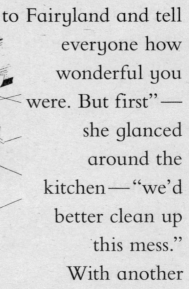 she glanced around the kitchen — "we'd better clean up this mess."

With another flick of Lizzie's wand, Rachel and Kirsty were returned to their human size.

Quickly, Kirsty picked up the chairs

the goblins had knocked over while Rachel found a broom to sweep up the silver balls. Meanwhile, Lizzie's fairy magic cleaned up

all the icing and clouds of flour from the walls and floor. The kitchen was spick and span in no time.

"What are we going to do about the goblins' cake?" Kirsty said, staring at the mess of cupcakes and icing on the cart. "We told Mrs. King we'd take it over to the Orangery."

Lizzie smiled. She flew over to the cake and a stream of fairy sparkles

swirled from her wand. The goblins'
blob of green cake and icing vanished.
In its place was an amazing golden-
colored palace-shaped cake with five
towers.

"It's the Golden Palace!" Rachel exclaimed with delight. "Look, Kirsty, the towers even have little paper flags on top of them."

"It's gorgeous!" Kirsty gasped.

"Enjoy your tea party, girls," Lizzie said with a smile. "Good-bye, and thank you again." Then she disappeared in a haze of fairy dust.

Rachel and Kirsty wheeled the cart with the Golden Palace cake on it over to the Orangery, where the tea party had already started. Everyone was sitting at the tables and a buzz of excited chatter filled the air.

"Ah, there you are, girls," said Mrs. King, coming to meet them. "Didn't the boys want to come to the party?"

Rachel shook her head. "No, they said they'd had too many sweet treats already!" she replied.

"Well, everyone here loves your rose petal decorations," Mrs. King told them. Then she noticed the cake and her eyes widened in amazement. "Goodness me, girls, that's wonderful!" Mrs. King declared. "A Golden Palace cake! I don't think I could have done better myself. You two certainly have the magic touch!"

Rachel and Kirsty laughed, and exchanged a secret smile. "We had a little help from our friends," Rachel told Mrs. King.

"Five fairy tiaras found," Kirsty whispered to Rachel. "And two to go!"

THE PRINCESS FAIRIES

Rachel and Kirsty have helped Hope,
Cassidy, Anya, Elisa, and Lizzie find their tiaras.
Now it's time for them to help

Maddie
the Fun and Games Fairy!

Join their next adventure
in this special sneak peek. . . .

A Face in the Bushes

"I've never seen such beautiful toys!" gasped Rachel Walker, gazing around with wide eyes.

"I can imagine the princes and princesses playing with them when they lived here long ago," agreed her best friend, Kirsty Tate.

The girls were standing in the royal playroom at the top of one of the Golden Palace's towers, where they were staying for a Royal Sleepover Camp. The other kids were already kneeling down beside the toys, choosing what they wanted to play with. There was a model steam engine that ran along a track around the room, a large jar full of swirly glass marbles, and boxes filled with puzzles and wooden spinning tops. Pretty china dolls sat on low shelves beside plump teddy bears, and balls of every size and color rolled around their feet.

"Oh, Rachel, look!" cried Kirsty.

On a low table in one corner of the room stood an exact miniature copy of the Golden Palace. It had the same gleaming white stone walls and golden turrets. Tiny flags fluttered from the top of each tower.

Rachel and Kirsty carefully opened the front wall to look inside. The rooms were exactly the same as those in the real palace, with thick carpets and plush furniture. There were dolls dressed in royal robes, as well as maids and butlers.

"This must be the princess," said Rachel, picking up a tiny girl doll with flowing golden hair and a sparkling tiara.

"She reminds me of Lizzie the Sweet Treats Fairy," whispered Kirsty.

The girls smiled at each other, thinking about their wonderful secret. They were good friends with the fairies, and often had magical adventures in Fairyland. . . .

RAINBOW magic

These activities are magical!
Play dress-up, send friendship notes, and much more!

SCHOLASTIC
www.scholastic.com
www.rainbowmagiconline.com

HIT entertainment

RMACTIV3

RAINBOW magic™

There's Magic in Every Series!

The Rainbow Fairies
The Weather Fairies
The Jewel Fairies
The Pet Fairies
The Fun Day Fairies
The Petal Fairies
The Dance Fairies
The Music Fairies
The Sports Fairies
The Party Fairies
The Ocean Fairies
The Night Fairies
The Magical Animal Fairies
The Princess Fairies

Read them all!

SCHOLASTIC

www.scholastic.com
www.rainbowmagiconline.com

HIT entertainment

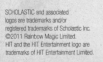
RMFAIRY